The Conch That Roared

The bizarre, true story of Key West's secession from the Union in 1982, its formation of the Conch Republic, and its declaration of war on the United States

Gregory King

Weston & Wright Publishing Company / Lexington, KY

First Printing 1997

Second Printing 1998, Revised

Publisher's Cataloging-in-Publication
(Provided by Quality Books, Inc.)

King, Gregory W.

The conch that roared: the bizarre, true story of Key West's
secession from the Union in 1982, its formation of the Conch
Republic, and its declaration of war on the United States /
Gregory King.

p. cm.
ISBN 0-9656932-6-0

1. Key West (Fla.)—History—1951-   I. Title

F319.K4K56 1997   975.9'41'063
                         QBI97-40289

Manufactured in the United States of America.

conch (konk) n. 1. Any of various tropical marine gastropod mollusks of the genus Strombus and other genera, having large, often brightly colored spiral shells and edible flesh— which writer Gini Alhadeff says tastes like "strips of elastic sea, bleached algae, mermaid hair, in mayonnaise." 2. A native of Key West, Florida.

Key West n. 1. "A place where the unexpected happens with monotonous regularity." (Benedict Thielen) 2. "The world's largest outdoor asylum." (Anon.) 3. "The place where you go when you don't want to grow up." (John "Butch" Robertson).

To Naples

Atlantic Ocean

Gulf of Mexico

Miami

Key West

Havana

CUBA

MIAMI 154

HAVANA 90

Key West

1

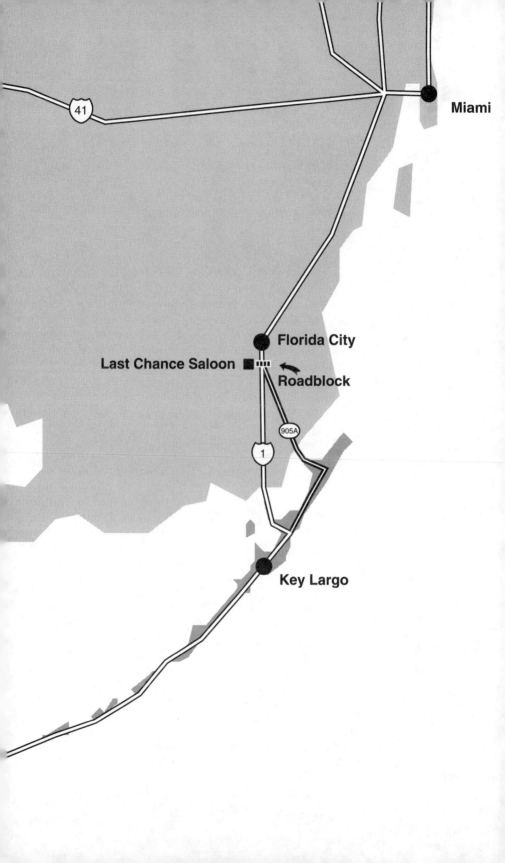

For Miki.

My best friend.

My partner.

My inspiration.

My wife.

Without whom ...

Had not these nice, generous people been willing to answer the author's stupid questions, correct his misconceptions, and share experiences and information from their files, you would probably be holding a greasy conch fritter right now instead of this Lilliputian book:

Peter W. Anderson, Secretary-General of the Conch Republic, Key West, FL.

C. Clyde Atkins, Chief United States District Judge (Senior Status), Southern District of Florida, Miami, FL.

Pamela Brown, Drug Enforcement Administration, Miami, FL.

Skeeter Dryer, Last Chance Saloon, Florida City, FL.

Grant (Grizzly) Gibbs, Four Geez Press, Roseville, CA.

United States Senator Bob Graham of Florida.

Tom Hambright, Monroe County Public Library, Key West, FL.

Wilhelmina Harvey, Monroe County Commissioner, Chief of the Armed Forces of the Conch Republic, Admiral of the Conch Republic Navy and First Sea Lord, Key West, FL.

David Paul Horan, Esq., Secretary of the Conch Republic Air Forces and Legal Counsel to the Conch Republic, Key West, FL.

Herbert Jefferson, United States Border Patrol, Miami, FL.

Joan Langley, Key West historian and accidental, clear-sighted, greatly appreciated editor of this work.

Wright Langley, Key West historian, Secretary of History of the Conch Republic, and valued advisor.

Lissette Nabut, The Miami Herald, Miami, FL.

Stuart Newman, Stuart Newman Associates Public Relations, Miami, FL.

Virginia Panico, Executive Director, Key West Chamber of Commerce.

Don Pinder, photographer, retired from the Key West Citizen, Key West, FL.

Robert A. Rosenberg, Assistant United States Attorney, Southern District of Florida, Fort Lauderdale, FL

Michael Sheehan, United States Customs Department, Miami, FL.

Edwin O. Swift III, Conch Republic Secretary of Transportation and principal of Historic Tours, Inc., operator of Key West's Old Town Trolley Tours and Shipwreck Historeum, Key West, FL.

And Dennis J. Wardlow, Mayor of Key West and Prime Minister of the Conch Republic.

FOREWORD

"Tiny Key West to Secede from Union"

—The Birmingham News
Friday, April 23, 1982

The year was 1982. Ronald Reagan was President. George Bush was Vice President. "Dallas" was the nation's most-watched television series. Apples were the hottest computers in the land. Kim Carnes' *Bette Davis Eyes* was the best-selling single record. The San Francisco 49ers won Super Bowl XVI. And the remote island city of Key West, Florida, seceded from the Union and proclaimed itself to be a free and independent nation called the Conch Republic. And then it declared war on the United States.

Seceded?!

Declared war?!

Why?!

And then what?!

You paid the outrageous price of this book for the answers to those tantalizing questions and, so, you shall have them. But, first, a little insight on the unique character and spirit of Key West, which may help you appreciate your answers more fully:

In her perennial best-seller The Florida Keys: A *History & Guide* (Random House), novelist and short story writer Joy Williams uses words like these to characterize Key West: peculiar, unlikely, charming, exasperating, seductive, dismaying, fanciful, zany, eclectic, seedy, urbane, freewheeling, lighthearted, gossipy, eccentric, excessive, and odd.

"It is a rather dirty town and has very little dignity," she adds, "but it has style."

Charles Kuralt agreed. In *Charles Kuralt's America* (G. P. Putnam's Sons), he said that Key West is "the greatest of all the end-of-the-road towns. This assures its lack of decorum, The Island is full of dreamers, drifters and drop-outs, spongers and idlers and barflies, writers and fishermen, islanders from the Caribbean and gays from the big cities, painters and pensioners, treasure hunters, real estate speculators, smugglers, runaways, old Conchs, and young lovers. The residents are all elaborately tolerant of one another, and that is where the style comes in."

PART I

"It's like 'The Mouse That Roared'"

—Ridgley Berger,
Key West clothing store owner,
at the secession ceremony on
Friday, April 23, 1982.
Reported by *The Miami Herald*.

Skeeter Dryer looked out a window of his Last Chance Saloon, just south of Florida City, and knew it was not going to be business as usual. This was on Sunday, April 18, 1982, at about 3:30 p.m. A number of Florida Highway Patrol troopers and shotgun-wielding agents of the United States Border Patrol were setting up a roadblock directly across from Dryer's bar, on U.S. Highway 1, the only road in and out of the Keys. Watching from unmarked sedans parked nearby were some somber-looking guys wearing polyester suits and sunglasses with reflective lenses. Dryer would later learn they were agents of the Drug Enforcement Administration (DEA).

When the barricades, flashing red lights, stop signs, and state troopers were in place, the heavy automobile traffic coming up from a fun-filled weekend in the Keys came to a halt in the sweltering afternoon sun. And the Border Patrol officers and polyester guys wearing sunglasses went to work. They began searching for "illegal aliens," they claimed. They demanded proof of U.S. citizenship from every driver, every passenger, then searched every vehicle; every engine compartment, every trunk, every piece of luggage, every glove compartment—which, as everybody knows, is the hiding place of choice for discerning illegal aliens.

Meanwhile, hundreds of vehicles, perhaps as many as 1,500, began to back up on the 19-mile stretch of desolate, uninhabited territory between the Last Chance Saloon and Key Largo.

In Key West, about 150 miles south, a blind amateur radio operator (ham) named Charles Wardlow was surfing the radio waves. He heard reports of the traffic jam from other hams who were trapped in it and may have discussed it with them, but nobody knew what was causing the snarl. To see if he could find out, or to sound a warning of potential trouble, Wardlow phoned his son Dennis, the mayor of Key West.

"I told Dad I had no idea what was going on," Dennis Wardlow recalled in the fall of 1996, near the end of his third and "final" term as Key West's mayor. "The blockade was news to me. But I said I'd check around and get back to him. Then I started burning up the phone lines, but I couldn't find out anything, mainly because it was a Sunday evening."

Later, back at the roadblock, the situation had turned ugly. *Real* ugly. Traffic was backed up for nearly 20 miles, all the way down to Key Largo. And many sweaty, thirsty, hungry, bathroom-deprived motorists, who had been waiting in the sun for up to five hours, had begun to hurl rocks, bottles, and other debris at Highway Patrol troopers. Other, even more exasperated motorists revolted and turned two-way U.S. 1 into a three-lane highway north by gunning their cars up the south-bound lane and on a shoulder, past the roadblock with their middle fingers extended vertically, and on to their destinations.

"It was big news that night, all over the television, shot from helicopters," Edwin O. (Ed) Swift III said in 1996. A successful real estate developer and an owner of Historic Tours Inc., the operator of Key West's Old Town Trolley Tours and Shipwreck Historeum, Swift was president of the Key West Chamber of Commerce when the roadblock was established.

"Cars were piled up all the way down past Key Largo," Swift added. "'The biggest parking lot in the nation,' reporters called it."

Early on the morning of Monday, April 19, Swift phoned Mayor Wardlow, a long-time friend. "'What the hell's going on?!' I said. 'This is terrible! Our economy's a mess, we're trying to develop tourism down here, and it's all over the country that there's a checkpoint up at Florida City! Stopping cars and searching them: hell, they don't even do that in a lot of European countries anymore!'"

Wardlow replied that he had not yet been able to learn anything beyond the fact that the checkpoint was a surprise Border Patrol action. "I couldn't find out who authorized it, though," Wardlow said. "All the officials I called said they didn't know anything about it. But I found out later what the deal was. The Border Patrol was working for the Reagan Administration's new Task Force on South

Florida Crime. Vice President Bush was heading it up, and
they didn't really care about illegal aliens, they were looking for drugs. It was all part of Reagan's War on Drugs."

Reagan's drug warriors had targeted the Keys because
drug smuggling there was a huge business and had been
since the early 1970s. By some accounts, an average of
150 tons of "Square Grouper" (bales of Mexican-grown
marijuana) each day were being smuggled into remote
Key West on boats made to look like fishing vessels. But
in 1982 marijuana was no longer Key West's most prof-
itable import. That honor had been usurped by cocaine,
the new Number One on America's hit parade of drugs.
And the DEA, frustrated in its efforts to stop the drug's
influx, had branded Key West as "The Drug Smuggling
Capital of America."

The chief Border Patrol agent in Miami, Robert Adams
Jr., must not have known that—because he told *The Miami
Herald* on April 19 that the purpose of the roadblock was
not to catch drug smugglers, but to collar illegal aliens.

Adams stuck to his story on April 20 when he told a
reporter for the *Key West Citizen*: "Our position is that we
have set up a checkpoint for illegal aliens. If anything else
came by, crime in other areas, we'd hold it, but this is primarily for illegal aliens." He added that his agency is the
enforcement arm of the Immigration and Naturalization
Service, and that his Miami contingent had recently been
boosted by Bush's task force from seven to 32 agents.

But whether vehicles were being searched for drugs or illegal aliens, or both, was not the burning issue for most of the citizens of the Keys. They were enraged because the federal government was treating the Keys like a foreign country. And Adams confirmed that conduct when he told *Newsweek* that "the roadblock is functioning as a national border."

"If the Border Patrol was that concerned with catching illegal aliens," Wardlow told the *Key West Citizen*, "they would put up roadblocks on Miami Beach or Fort Lauderdale, where the Haitians are landing, and quit picking on the Keys. They're always picking on us, and I'm very disgusted."

Monroe County Commissioner Curt Blair agreed. "We have done nothing but suffer from problems generated by the federal government," he said, referring to the roadblock, the 1973 closing of a Navy base that had been Key West's largest employer, and the Mariel boatlift, which destroyed the tourism season of 1980.

(In the spring of 1980, President Jimmy Carter announced that the U.S. would open its arms and heart to Cubans seeking freedom from Fidel Castro's Communist dictatorship. Big mistake. Over 125,000 refugees—an estimated 23,000 of whom were dumped from Castro's prisons and mental asylums—massed at the island's Mariel Harbor and had to be ferried to Key West in a fleet of American fishing boats, yachts, and sailboats known as the "Freedom

Flotilla." Most of these exiles, called "Marielitos," now live in Miami.)

William E. (Bill) Smith, Executive Director of the Greater Key West Chamber of Commerce, said to a *Miami Herald* reporter: "It's like making us third-class citizens. We're citizens of the United States. It's not right for them to set up a separate border in the Keys. We shouldn't be subject to search and seizure every time we want to get in or out of the county."

Richard Heyman, a Key West City Commissioner, then asked the 64-dollar question: "Since when is Florida City a border? They should be checking all along the shoreline where these people (Haitians and Cubans) come into the country, not Florida City."

Phone calls from reporters throughout the country started pouring into Wardlow's office soon after his early-morning conversation with Ed Swift. "They all wanted to know what was going on," Wardlow said. "Is it another Mariel boatlift? Were we being invaded?" And by the end of the day, every major city in America knew about the Border Patrol's roadblock at Florida City.

"The message it was sending to tourists," Swift said, "was 'don't go to the Keys!'"

And they got the message loud and clear. Room reservations in Key West began to be canceled at an alarming rate.

"It's a deterrent to coming to the Keys if there's a line of traffic," the Chamber's Bill Smith said to *The Miami Herald*. "We object to this, and the Chamber is drafting a resolution protesting the patrol checkpoint. It's going to be sent to our senators and congressmen in Washington."

Rick Easton, marketing director for the Pier House Resort, underscored Smith's comment. "The winter season is over and now the city relies on tourists coming down by car. They're not going to want to go down to the Keys if it means waiting in line eight hours to get home. Two years ago this week was the Mariel thing. Just when we're building up some positive publicity, then this happens."

"If this is continued," added Dennis Bitner, a member of Key West's Tourist Development Commission and owner of the Club Key West guest house, "we're going to see a 40-percent reduction in tourism this summer. And without South Florida money in the summertime, we're dead."

"We're dead." Those words could have been echoing in Wardlow's head when he got the Border Patrol chief on the phone in Miami and pled the Keys' case: they felt they were being treated like a foreign country and the roadblock was ruining their tourism-based economy.

But Adams denied the Keys any relief. He said his agency was going to keep stopping cars "seven days a week, 24 hours a day." However, he would issue an apology for the previous evening's traffic catastrophe caused by the roadblock—which netted 11 people who were charged with being illegal aliens and two U.S. citizens who were nabbed for having 150 pounds of marijuana in their possession. Only one of the people charged with being an illegal alien, a Chilean, was found to have entered the United States through the Keys.

"We regret the inconvenience and pledge that there will be no major delays in the future," Adams told reporters later that day. "We do ask the public for its indulgence during this very necessary program ... Any delays resulting from future checkpoint operations will be brief. We hope to keep them to less than 45 minutes."

That didn't satisfy Wardlow one bit. In fact, he said it only made him angrier. So he fired off telegrams to Vice President Bush, Florida's Governor Bob Graham, its U.S. senators and congressmen, and all the state legislators he could think of.

"Urgent," the telegrams read. "Request lift roadblock on U.S. 1 at Florida City. Having adverse effects on Keys tourism."

Florida Congressman Dante B. Fascell reacted to Wardlow's telegram by phoning Rodger Brandenmuehl, Chief of the U.S. Border Patrol in Washington. Brandenmuehl said he was "extremely chagrined" over the traffic tie-up Sunday and promised it would not happen again, according to a report by United Press International (UPI). Nevertheless, he said the Border Patrol would continue the road block for two weeks and then evaluate its effectiveness.

U.S. Senator Bob Graham of Florida, then Governor Graham, said that he and several members of his staff, alerted by news reports on Sunday evening, had already begun an investigation of the "roadblock problem" when they received Wardlow's telegram. "I told Dennis I would see what could be done about it and let him know," Graham said.

The first admission that the roadblock was actually a front for a DEA crackdown on drug smugglers, and not a Border Patrol attempt to snag illegal aliens, came astonishingly from the DEA itself. In defending the blockade, spokesman Con Dougherty casually told a *Miami Herald* reporter that "it will be useful in the fight against drug smugglers, even if smart smugglers hold back. After all, it is a deterrent."

But Peter Teeley, Vice President Bush's press secretary, stuck fast to the illegal alien story. In his defense of the roadblock, he said, "It's regrettable but necessary. You can't have it both ways. You have illegal aliens and crime on the streets. You want the illegal aliens picked up? There's going to be some inconvenience.

"I think most people would want a little inconvenience compared to having grocery stores held up and senior citizens mugged in the streets."

Not Dennis Wardlow. He and the Keys had had it up to their eyeballs in inconvenience. They feared there would be more to come, much more. And they had no confidence that politicians were going to be able to save their butts from financial ruin. So, on Tuesday, April 20, Wardlow scheduled the first of what would be three "brainstorming sessions" with the men who, along with himself, were destined to become the founding fathers of the Conch Republic: Ed Swift and Bill Smith of the Chamber of Commerce, Dennis Bitner of the Key West Tourist Development Commission, John Magliola, the general manager and part owner of radio station WIIS (Island 107FM), and

Townsend Kieffer, a writer and civic activist.

The meeting was held at Magliola's radio station, in a small room used for the production of commercials. "We met out of frustration over not being able—even as the mayor of Key West, or the president of the Chamber of Commerce, or anybody—to get any information out of the government," Swift recalled. "It was one those things that just sticks in your craw. You become so damned pissed off that these people can do this to you without a word of warning, without any explanation, without any rationale. And to this day, I don't think anybody has come up with the reason they did it. It was probably just a bunch of agents sitting around some saloon in Miami and deciding to do it. And George Bush, poor guy, I don't think he had a clue about why they did it."

(At press time, President Bush had not responded to phone calls and letters of inquiry about this earth-shaking matter. But you can bet your bippie that he knew exactly what his Ray-Banned minions were up to in the Keys in 1982. After all, he was Vice President at the time and was previously [1976 to 1977] Director of the Central Intelligence Agency. The only mystery is why such a smart and well-informed man would sanction such dumb-ass activities.)

Now, back to the studios of WIIS.

One of the first and certainly most important decisions made at that initial meeting of Swift, Wardlow, Magliola,

Smith, Bitner, and Kieffer was to hire an attorney to deter-
mine if the Border Patrol's "illegal or at least grossly unfair"
actions could be stopped by an injunction, Swift said.

The attorney tapped for the job was David Paul Horan,
who three months earlier had become Monroe County's
first attorney in the 21st century to argue a case before the
U.S. Supreme Court. Using the Constitution of the
United States as a shield, he had protected the wreck of
the Spanish galleon *Santa Margarita* and its multi-million-
dollar treasure—the first of treasure hunter Mel Fisher's
great discoveries—from the covetous hands of the State of
Florida, which had conspired with the federal government
to take possession of them.

Horan was retained by the Key West Chamber of
Commerce, the City of Key West, the Key West Hotel and
Motel Association, and Dennis Wardlow, individually and
as Mayor of Key West.

Later that day, Horan told reporters he believed that
the Border Patrol's roadblock constituted "unreasonable
search and seizure."

"The Fourth Amendment of the Constitution says they
have to have probable cause to search," the attorney
explained. "Unless they see the hand of a Haitian sticking
out of the trunk, or marijuana wafting out of the car, they
don't have probable cause."

The Fourth Amendment reads, in part:

"The right of the people to be secure in their persons,

houses, papers and effects, against unreasonable searches and seizures, shall not be violated ..."

"What the feds are acting on," Horan continued, "is the 'doctrine of functional equivalency.' They're taking the position that the roadblock is the functional equivalent of a border. But there isn't a border there, and all the people going through are U.S. citizens. It's the degree of interference with free travel that's at issue."

Horan added that he had enlisted the help of Florida State University law professor John Yetter in researching the case and scheduled a hearing before a U.S. District Judge at 2 p.m. on Thursday, April 22, which was two days away.

You will soon learn that Horan claimed to have discovered evidence of government deception and abuse of power, and later alleged that the legal system had been manipulated by none other than Attorney General William French Smith. But, first, let us examine the BIG IDEA and its origin.

The BIG IDEA, which was to be acted upon if Horan failed to get an injunction against the Border Patrol, was this:

Key West was to demonstrate its outrage over being treated so shabbily by the federal government—and perhaps turn adversity into opportunity—by symbolically seceding from the Union and proclaiming itself to be the Conch Republic, then declaring war on the United States, surrendering immediately, and applying to the United Nations for $1 billion in foreign aid.

History has shown that this was one of the great publicity stunts of all time; a classic public relations spin of heart-pounding disaster into giddy good fortune; a spectacular melange of showmanship, hucksterism, and determination that would have made P.T. Barnum proud. So, naturally, there are a number of people who claim to have thought it up, although who did so doesn't seem to matter much in the grand scheme of things.

Nevertheless, "There are so many people who claim that the secession was their idea that, if we lined them all up, they would stretch from one end of the island to the other," said Peter W. Anderson, Secretary-General of the Conch Republic and the maestro of Conch Republic Days, Key West's annual celebration of its independence.

This was confirmed by a lengthy investigation that mercifully led this reporter into most of the 126 bars on Key West. Along the way, which became perilous at times, 16 men and two women said the secession was their idea. Also, a wild-eyed guy claimed that the CIA had recently swapped his brain with that of Cuban dictator Fidel Castro, and a young, pregnant woman said tearfully that the father of her child-to-be was "a gentle visitor from that constellation right over there, Pleiades."

In the final analysis, however, it turns out there are only seven people who can legitimately lay claim to THE

BIG IDEA. Six of them are bright, creative guys who worked shoulder to shoulder during the border crisis and were almost entirely responsible for saving Key West from being strangled by the federal government. They are, of course, the Six Concheteers: Dennis Wardlow, Ed Swift, John Magliola, Dennis Bitner, Bill Smith, and Townsend Kieffer. The seventh person is a bright, creative guy named Stuart Newman, a Miami publicist who had been representing the Monroe County Tourist Development Council for two years when the roadblock was established.

"I received a call from Dennis Wardlow the morning after the roadblock was put up," Newman recalled. "He told me about all the problems it was causing and asked me if I had any ideas about what to do about it. I said, 'Dennis, you're forgetting your own history.' He said, 'What do you mean?'

"I had remembered that, a month or two before, a writer with *National Geographic* was down here researching a story on Florida and he came in and talked with me about the Keys. And in that process I had done a little research and discovered that, during the Civil War, when Florida had seceded from the Union, Key West had seceded from Florida. The reason was that there was a garrison of Union troops in Key West, at Ft. Zachary Taylor, and they didn't want Key West to be part of the Confederacy. So, I mentioned that to Dennis. Then I said, 'Dennis why don't you just do what your people did 150 years ago? Why don't you secede from the Union?' He said, 'Are you crazy? We can't do that!' I said, 'Of course, you can't do it officially, but you can do a mock secession.' And then they got caught up in the idea and came up with the Conch Republic name, and the rest is history. The Keys like nothing better than a party and that gave them an excuse for one.

"From a public relations standpoint," Newman concluded, "we look at it as a classic example of creating an opportunity out of a near disaster."

OK, now that you know who hatched THE BIG IDEA, let's go back to the Last Chance Saloon where this epic began. The joint was being turned into a disaster area by the Border Patrol's roadblock. Owner Skeeter Dryer, who claimed he had lost $50,000 and almost his entire business during the Mariel boatlift fiasco of 1980, said it was déjà vu all over again.

But from the standpoint of the Border Patrol and Highway Patrol, everything was hunky-dory. "There were no problems tonight (Monday), it's going a lot smoother," a border patrolman told UPI, adding that no more illegal aliens or drug smugglers had been apprehended. The Highway Patrol agreed that traffic was "virtually unimpeded" by the roadblock.

"And I was dying," Dryer recalled. "With the law and the roadblock being there, people had difficulty getting in and out of the bar, or were put off by the situation. So things were real slow during the day and I didn't realize any night business at all. After five o'clock, that expensive nightclub license I pay Dade County for wasn't doing me a bit of good."

So Dryer got "fighting mad" and started organizing business people in the Upper Keys to sue the federal government. He also began offering travelers a hot-line advisory on checkpoint activities by putting up a large sign in front of his business that read ROAD BLOCK INN, BORDER HOTLINE, 248-4935.

"I became Checkpoint Charlie," Dryer said. "Every time somebody wanted to know if the checkpoint was up, they'd give me a call. Or I'd call Dennis Wardlow and let him know what was going on. Of course, the whole point of it

©1997 by Murry H. Sill

Skeeter Dryer, a Conch Republic patriot through and through, stands near where the infamous roadblock was established in 1982

was ridiculous. Every illegal alien and drug smuggler in the country knew about the checkpoint. It was all over the news. What are you going to do, sit in line for hours waiting for the Border Patrol to check out the illegal aliens and drugs in your trunk? That's why the highway was littered with drugs at that time, marijuana and stuff that people threw out of their cars before they got to the roadblock. And all that got picked up by the guys from the prison camp down the road who were supposed to be keeping the roadside clean."

Thursday, April 22, 1982: Attorney David Paul Horan was ready for action in U.S. District Court.

"We had done an incredible amount of research and work in a very brief period of time," he recalled in 1996. "We had learned some interesting things and figured out what the government was up to.

"I have to say that I have almost a knee-jerk dislike for government. I think it's a necessary evil. It's kind of like castor oil; you don't need a full dose of it if you need just a little help. But the government doesn't know how to do anything in moderation. Bureaucrats abhor a legislative vacuum. If they see something that's not totally regulated, that's a vacuum to be filled with regulations.

"But that's sort of beside the point. The situation was that we were in the middle of some real bad problems with regard to drugs coming into the Keys. William French Smith, who was then Attorney General of the United

States, was committed to doing everything he possibly could to stop it. He wanted to put a DEA roadblock at Florida City and search every car coming up from the Keys, but he couldn't do that because the DEA can't search without a warrant. They've got to have probable cause.

"Then [Smith] learned about a case that the Border Patrol had won out in California, a case called *Gonzales*. It allowed for a 'displaced threshold' from a border, for border searches. What was happening was that there were dozens of places along the Mexican border where illegal aliens could come across; too many places for the Border Patrol to possibly cover. But eventually those illegals would come together at a main highway, get picked up by transporters, and then hauled up to the population centers where they could get work. So the United States decided it was OK for the Border Patrol to establish a station 50 to 70 miles up the highway from the actual border and search vehicles without warrants

"Well, Smith said, 'Aha! That's how we can do it. We can use the Border Patrol, which can search without warrants, to set up a roadblock that doesn't have to be on a border. And we can have the DEA there, looking over their shoulders for drugs.' And that's exactly what they did at Florida city.

"Once I figured out what they were up to, that they were operating the roadblock in the guise of a displaced threshold, it became clear that was not the intent of the

Gonzales case. So I knew I could win by distinguishing Gonzales from what they were doing, which was abusing the law. And I came up with the evidence to prove it.

"There was a young attorney and his date who had been down in the Keys. They were in a Camaro and had been stopped at the roadblock. Channel 7 (WSNV-TV in Miami) was there, getting it all on tape. A border patrol agent asked them to get out of the car so it could be searched and the attorney asked, 'What probable cause do you have to search my car?' The border patrolman said, 'We don't need probable cause.' So he got out of the car and they said, 'Open the trunk.' He said, 'No.' They said, 'Give us your keys! We're going to search your trunk!' He said, 'No, you don't have probable cause. I'm not going to allow you to search.' Then they said, 'We don't need your keys!' And they popped his trunk with a crowbar. And at that point, he became furious and started using some inappropriate language. And Channel 7 had it all on tape, which showed clearly that they were searching without probable cause.

"So, anyway, we had all this information and knew we could stop the roadblock. We could prove that the DEA was using the Border Patrol to make warrantless searches. It was so damned transparent, it was just incredible. So, I went ahead and filed the suit. We filed it as an emergency and got a hearing before a federal judge in Miami. And then something very unusual happened. At the very last minute, the case was transferred to the *chief* federal judge, Clyde Atkins. So I thought, 'Goddam, that's really interesting. Why would they do that?' And I found out why."

But Horan didn't find out what he said he "found out" until after the April 22nd hearing, so neither will you, anxious reader.

It was sunny, clear, and 85 degrees on the morning of the 22nd. Horan, Dennis Wardlow, Ed Swift, John Magliola, and Virginia Panico drove to Key West International Airport, clambered into Horan's twin-engine AeroStar, and flew to Miami. Panico was head of Key West's Hotel-Motel Association and is now Executive Director of the Chamber of Commerce.

"We were really fired up," Horan said. "We had the Channel 7 videotape, we had witnesses, we had photographs, and we had been up till the wee small hours of the morning getting ready. So we got up to the courtroom, the case was called, and Judge Atkins says, 'Before we start this hearing, I understand that the Assistant U.S. Attorney (Robert A. Rosenberg) has a brief statement he would like to make to the court.'

"And then the judge called on this fellow, who got up and said, 'Well, we know there's been a few problems in the past, and there have been some overly zealous officers involved. Now, we're not admitting that any of the allegations that have been made against us are correct, but we aren't going to operate the checkpoint the same way anymore. We're going to let the normal flow of traffic go by and check only a small number of cars periodically in a displaced area. And the only thing we'll ask the drivers is to see their licenses, or some other form of identification. And unless there's probable cause to believe the law is being violated, we will not search their cars or their person.' And then he said, 'We believe these things will take care of all the plaintiffs' problems with regard to the checkpoint.'

"Then Judge Atkins looks over at me and says, 'Well, I think that's a tremendous show of good faith, don't you, Mr. Horan?' And I said, 'But it's not an injunction, your honor. Are they agreeing to an injunction against them on these terms?' And the judge says, 'Well, I don't believe that they're having to agree to an injunction. And I'm not sure that the court's power is necessary when he (Rosenberg) represents that they're going to change their methods of operation.'

"This was the chief judge of the federal Southern District of Florida talking to me; a judge who was appointed for life; one of the most powerful men in the United States. And he says to me, 'Here's the way I think we ought to resolve this. If they don't do exactly what they have said they're going to do—if they continue to cause traffic backups, if they continue to search without probable cause, if they don't have a displaced area for their investigations—all you need to do is call this office and I'll immediately issue the injunction. But I don't believe that the injunction is necessary at this point. Now, don't you think that's a good way to resolve this?'

"And I said, 'We're ready for the hearing, your honor.' He said, 'We're not going to have a hearing. That's the way this is going to be resolved.'"

Period. End of argument. Judge Atkins said the economic impact of the roadblock on Key West's tourist industry was "regretful," but still he ruled that the checkpoint was a legal "administrative decision" by the Border Patrol. And that was that. *Finis.*

OK, now here's what Horan said he "found out" about why his case was transferred to Judge Atkins' courtroom:

"The fix was in."

Horan explained that, soon after the hearing, he learned that Attorney General William French Smith had flown into Miami prior to the hearing and met with Judge Atkins. He said Smith was concerned about the negative and embarrassing publicity that would be generated by an injunction against the Vice President's Task Force on Drugs, so he "worked out his fallback position" with Judge Atkins.

"And his fallback position was exactly what the U.S. Attorney read into the record," Horan added. "So, my clients turned to me and said, 'Did we win?' And I said, 'Well, it's kind of like a kiss from your sister. It's nice, but it isn't exactly what a kiss is supposed to be. And I'm sorry but, no, I don't think we won. I think they did an end run around us.'

"But we did get the relief we wanted. We got the ability to say that there wouldn't be anymore lengthy traffic jams as a result of the roadblock. But we didn't get the publicity we needed to tell the nation that we were open for business again. And that's what we were looking for."

Minutes later, however, Horan and his clients walked out onto the steps of the courthouse and ignited a wildfire of national publicity. But before we join them, let's go back for a moment to Horan's allegation that "the fix was in."

This is a serious charge, folks. If it's true, Judge Atkins' sterling reputation could be tarnished severely. Unfortunately, the judge, now 83, was unavailable for comment when the first edition of this book went to press in February 1997; he was recovering from a fall. Attorney General William French Smith died in 1990. So, without either of the principal players in this comedy-drama available to deny or confirm Horan's accusation, Senator Bob Graham, a long-time friend of Judge Atkins, was asked for his opinion.

"I had not heard that story before," Senator Graham said. "I know Judge Atkins fairly well. He is now in senior status, but was a federal District Judge in Miami for the better part of 30 years. He was the principal judge in many of the desegregation cases and is very highly respected, able, and if there is one quality that most characterizes him it is solidly independent. If that conversation took place, I would have liked to have been a fly on the wall and heard what Judge Atkins said."

Assistant U.S. Attorney Robert A. Rosenberg—the very same Robert A. Rosenberg who represented the federal government in Judge Atkins' courtroom on the morning of April 22, 1982, and still maintains that the Florida City roadblock was set up to catch illegal aliens, not drug smugglers—distilled his opinion of Horan's charge down to a single word:

"Baloney!"

Speaking from his Ft. Lauderdale office in April 1997, Rosenberg went on to say that he had no knowledge of William French Smith being in Miami at the time of the hearing, that neither he nor anybody in the Florida offices of the Justice Department had any contact with the Attorney General at that time, and that he was certain that Judge Atkins had not had any contact with the man.

"So, if he (Horan) is saying that a fix was in," Rosenberg concluded, "it may be to sensationalize the story. But I don't know what he's talking about. It doesn't make any sense to me. It's totally inconsistent with the way I was proceeding in the case."

Several days later, a response from Judge Atkins finally arrived in the form of a letter. "Dear Mr. King," it read, "I have sent a copy of your letter [which outlined Horan's allegation] to Mr. Horan for his input.

"Your letter implies an 'ex parte' conversation between Mr. Smith and me in 1982. [An *ex parte* conversation is one from which the adverse party is excluded.] I have had a firm policy from the very beginning of my service in August 1966 on the District Court Bench never to engage in an 'ex parte' conversation with counsel or a party in litigation. I frequently have joint conferences with counsel for all sides and interests, usually in the courtroom with a court reporter present. Perhaps your description of Mr. Horan's comment was not intended to indicate a personal 'ex parte' request by Mr. Smith. Of course, parties can make requests, though counsel, in open court or by written motions or at a joint conference. Thereafter, formal written Orders are entered reflecting rulings by the Court emanating from such joint conferences. Occasionally, I hold joint telephone conferences with counsel. Any such rulings made at such conferences are likewise reflected in a written Order subsequently entered and filed.

"I hope I have made clear that I am quite sure no 'ex parte' conversation was held with Mr. Smith or his representative.

"Sincerely yours, C. Clyde Atkins."

Judge Atkins sent copies of this letter to Senator Graham and Horan, who phoned shortly after receiving his to amend his previous statements.

"I don't know whether he (Judge Atkins) met with him (U.S. Attorney General William French Smith) or not,"

Horan admitted. "All I could do is deduce it from these points that are absolutely, totally clear:

"The case, which was generating a lot of publicity, had been transferred in a very short period of time from the original judge [to whom it had been assigned] to the Chief Judge, who was C. Clyde Atkins, OK?

"I knew that William French Smith had flown into Miami the day before, OK?

"Then I have everything ready and I go into the court-room, and ... he (Atkins) says, before we can get started, 'I think he (Rosenberg) has something to say. Then the guy (Rosenberg) goes through this narrative and, when he fin-ishes, Judge Atkins does not ask him a single question, not one. He turned to me and said, 'Well I think that's really good faith,' and on and on and on. OK?

"Now, my assumption at that point was that Judge Atkins did not have a premonition that the U.S. Attorney was going to make a presentation when he walked into that courtroom. Somebody had to tell the judge, 'There's going to be a presentation.'

"Based on those assumptions, I believed that ... they had made their deal. I don't know that they *made* the deal. I can't say because I wasn't there and, certainly, I could not have known whether he (Atkins) had a personal conversa-tion with William French Smith, or whether one of William French Smith's people was working with his law clerk. But it seemed to me that somebody had told him that there was going to be a presentation by the U.S. Attorney prior to him walking into court that day."

Now to the front steps of the U.S. District Court in Miami when Horan and his clients emerged into the media circus that had been arranged by John Magliola.

"When we walked out," Ed Swift recalled, "I was flabbergasted. John (Magliola) had said he could get us some press, but that was an understatement. There was more press outside that courthouse than I've ever seen in my life. TV cameras and microphones, and reporters were everywhere. Dozens of them. It looked like something out of one of those movies where the guy comes out of court and everybody's sticking microphones in his face. Well, poor Dennis (Wardlow), they're sticking microphones and cameras, and lights in his face, and asking him all kinds of questions about what went on in court."

"I told the reporters that we had won somewhat of a victory," Wardlow said, "but not a total victory, because the Border Patrol was still insisting that it was going to make the checkpoint permanent. So then I unfolded a Key West flag I had with me and held it out so everybody could see it, and said we were going to secede at noon the next day and run that flag up the pole and become the Conch Republic. And that's how it all got started."

Horan recalled the very first act of insurrection. "When we left Miami that day, we flew over to the roadblock and dived down and buzzed it. Then we came back here and had a rebellion. And it was one of the funniest things I've ever been through."

Friday, April 23, 1982: Key West Independence Day. Wardlow's phone began to ring angrily at 6 a.m. "It was Admiral McKenzie, who was in command of the Navy base here. He said, 'Dennis, what the hell are you doing?! I've got Secret Service agents calling me, I've got FBI agents calling! They don't know whether to arrest you, or laugh with you, because they say you're going to take down the American flag, then declare war on the U.S. and shoot at our ships!'"

Admiral McKenzie's was but the first of many calls Wardlow received that morning from patriotic individuals and groups, such as the Veterans of Foreign Wars (VFW) and Daughters of the American Revolution (DAR), who were outraged by news reports like this one from the previous day's edition of the *Key West Citizen*:

"Tomorrow at 11 a.m. the Florida Keys will secede from the Union in ceremonies at Old Town Square with the red, white and blue being lowered, the Key West flag being raised and the formal declaration of the Conch Republic being sent to Washington."

Wardlow claimed that this report and others, particularly that of the widely circulated *Miami Herald*, stated incorrectly that the "red, white and blue" was going to be lowered at the secession ceremonies.

"I had made it very clear from the beginning that we

would do absolutely nothing to desecrate the American flag or embarrass the United States," Wardlow said. "I had made it clear we were going to have a *mock* secession. But some of the reporters didn't get it right for some reason—which caused us a lot of problems. And I told Admiral McKenzie that. I assured him that there was no intention of lowering the American flag; that it wouldn't even be present when we raised the flag of the Conch Republic."

This appeased the admiral, Wardlow said, but still he had to cope with all the other people who had been stirred up by the newspaper reports. "Somebody who said he was a veteran called and said he was going to shoot me if I lowered the flag. Some of the politicians in the upper Keys said they didn't want to have anything to do with it; Key West was on its own. Some of my own city commissioners said I was nuts for seceding, that I was committing political suicide, probably get run out of town. An old man called and wanted to know if Social Security would still be in effect. Somebody else called and wanted to know if American money was going to be any good in the Conch Republic. And press from all over the country was calling every five minutes. It was pretty hairy between that six o'clock call from Admiral McKenzie and noon. Truthfully, I was worried. I didn't know if I'd made the right decision or not."

High noon at Old Town Square on Wall Street: More than 700 Key Westers and clueless tourists—wearing everything from bathing suits to business suits—were crowded around an old flatbed trailer that had been parked beside a flagpole near the entrance to the Chamber of Commerce. Some were drinking *Cuba Libres* (rum, cola, and Key Lime juice). Others were waving miniature Conch Republic flags, bumper stickers that said "Border Pass" and "Conch Republic Visa," and placards saying "Remember the Aloe" and "Don't Tread on Conchs." And others, many others, were wielding video cameras, still cameras, and microphones with which they were going to record the oddly sensational event for the news media they represented.

Key West was doing what it does best—it was partying—so the mood of the crowd generally was festive. But there were protesters, indignant poster-wavers who still didn't realize that the secession was a gigantic, quasi-serious put-on. Among them were members of the VFW and DAR, the Elks Lodge, and a few local politicos, all of whom later got the joke and embraced the rebellion.

"When I got there," Wardlow recalled, "I saw all these protesters and plainclothes police in the crowd, and there were some others, government types, and navy personnel. I thought I was going to be arrested, or tarred and feathered."

The secession ceremony was kicked off by Chamber of Commerce President Ed Swift. He climbed up onto the flatbed, grabbed the microphone of a public address system and began to speak.

(What Swift and others said was recorded by historian Joan Langley and transcribed for this account. The speakers' remarks have been edited for clarity and brevity.)

"Nice to see all you beautiful people here today," Swift said. "The Mayor of Key West will be out here in just a minute. But, first, I want to say that at no time have we meant any disrespect to the American flag."

Pointing to Old Glory, which was waving from a pole across the square, Swift continued. "The American flag is flying high and beautifully, and we salute it. We do, however, wish—and by this ceremony we hope to call attention to the fact—that we feel that the federal government has hurt us citizens of Monroe County, stepped on us.

"Yesterday, we went before Judge Atkins in Federal Court in Miami and he said, basically, that the Border Patrol is out of line. It hasn't followed its own rules and regulations for setting up a checkpoint, and did not adequately consider the safety of the people of Monroe County in setting up the checkpoint at Florida City. He did not give us the restraining order we were after, but he did assure us that we would not have any more than two weeks of this border checkpoint, that there would be only sporadic checks, that the free flow of traffic would not be hindered, and that no more cars would be searched illegally. The judge also said to notify him if this outrage of backing up cars and blockading our roads ever occurs again.

"You would have been very proud of the attorney for the Chamber of Commerce and Hotel and Motel Association, Dave Horan, who did a super job. And you would have been proud of your mayor, who stood up there on the stand and told it like it was. Our mayor and soon-to-be Prime Minister of the Conch Republic, Mr. Dennis Wardlow!"

Wardlow got up onto the flatbed and took the microphone from Swift. "I want everyone to know first off that this is a mock secession," he said. "I say this because a rumor that we were going to take down the American flag got started and that has really hurt me. We would never do such a thing. We all love America. We're good Americans and we wouldn't do anything to hurt the American flag. We're here today to have a good time and we just hope everyone takes this in that spirit.

"You know why we're here, of course. We're here because of the Border Patrol's refusal to remove the check station, which insults us because it accuses us of smuggling drugs and aliens. So in protest, we're making a mock secession from the Union today. We're going to become the Conch Republic.

"But, first, I want to say that we are tired of our county being ignored by the state and by our senators and congressmen because we have so few votes. And that's about to change, because as a new nation, as the Conch Republic, we'll have 100 percent of the votes!

Mayor Dennis Wardlow, center, took the microphone and
declared Key West's independence.

"We were once the richest town south of Savannah.
Now, we're just the highest taxed, highest in living
expenses, and highest on the list of towns to be ignored by

the politicians in Washington. This city has had more ups and downs in the past 160 years than any part of the United States. We've gone through the sponge war, the cigar labor riots, the Depression, and the Navy pull-out. Then we had the Mariel boatlift, courtesy of President Carter. And, now, the roadblock with armed agents of the federal government stopping cars and threatening those who leave the Florida Keys as though they're returning from a foreign country.

"So if Key West is a foreign country to Washington, Washington shall represent a foreign nation to Key West! Raise the flag of the Conch Republic!"

Accompanied by riotous cheering, whistling, and applause, the sky-blue, conch-pink, and sun-yellow flag of the Conch Republic was run up the flagpole beside the flatbed trailer. Wardlow then read from a prepared statement.

"We, the people of Key West, are called Conchs. Sometimes we are called Conchs with affection, sometimes with humor, and sometimes with derision.

"I proclaim that Key West shall now be known as the Conch Republic and, as the flag of our new republic is raised, I hereby state to Washington and the rest of the United States, and the world, what the Conchs are and were.

"When Jamestown, Virginia, was settled by Englishmen who were fed up with the arrogance, the derision, the

Birth of a new nation.

abuse of rights by a despot, a king without compassion or sense of humanity, another group was settling in the Bahamas and they were called 'Conchs.'

"They were known as Conchs because they hoisted flags with the tough, hard conch shellfish on them, indicating they'd rather eat conch than pay the king's taxes and live under his tyranny.

"There's our flag. It has a conch on it. We secede from

the United States. We've raised our flag, given our notice, and named our new government.

"We serve notice on the government in Washington to remove the roadblock or get ready to put up a permanent border to a new foreign land.

"We as people may have suffered in the past, but we have no intention of suffering in the future at the hands of fools and bureaucrats.

"We're not going to beg, to beseech the nation of the United States for help. We're not going to ask for something we should naturally have as citizens, simple equality.

"If we are not equal, we'll get out. It's as simple as that.

"The first step was, like Mariel, up to Washington. This step is up to us.

"We call upon other people of the Florida Keys to join us or not, as they see fit. We're not a fearful people. We're not a group to cringe and whimper when Washington cracks the whip with contempt and unconcern.

"We're Conchs and we've had enough. We're happy to secede today with some humor. But there's some anger, too.

"Big trouble has started in much smaller places than this.

"I am calling on all my fellow citizens here in the Conch Republic to stand together, lest we fall apart; fall from fear, from a lack of courage, intimidation by an uncaring government whose actions show it has grown too big to care for people on a small island. "Long live the Conch Republic!"

Ed Swift then led the crowd in three rousing cheers for Wardlow. Afterward, he introduced the Conch Republic's Minister of Defense, City Commissioner Joe Balbotin, who outlined the Republic's military strategy against the United States.

"I'm ready to declare war!" shouted the stocky plumbing contractor. "I'm ready to take over the territorial waters of the Conch Republic from the U.S. Navy! For ammunition, we will use all the hard Cuban bread we can find and shoot it at them!"

And that's just what Balbotin did next, according to Ed Swift. "There was a uniformed navy officer there and we asked him if he'd come up on the trailer and he said, 'OK.' And he jumps up there and Joe Balbotin hit him with a loaf of stale Cuban bread and said, 'We've fired a shot! Now we're at war with the United States!' Then he handed the bread to the navy officer and said, 'Now we surrender!'"

When the laughter and applause died down, Wardlow took the microphone and said: "We've read our proclamation seceding, we've fired our volley, we've surrendered. Now we're going to apply for a billion dollars in foreign aid from the United Nations!"

Ridgley Berger, a clothing store owner in the crowd, turned to a reporter from *The Miami Herald*. "It's like 'The Mouse That Roared,'" he said, referring to the 1959 movie starring Peter Sellers. "Just like 'The Mouse That Roared.'"

PART II

"We seceded where others failed"

—Official motto of the
Conch Republic, coined by
Peter W. Anderson, Secretary-
General of the Conch Republic

"Governor, I have some disquieting news. Key West has just seceded from the Union." With those words, a state policeman greeted Governor Bob Graham when his plane landed at Key West International Airport on the afternoon of the secession.

"I was to be the commencement speaker at Florida Keys Community College the next afternoon," Graham recalled. "So I flew down from Tallahassee and a state law enforcement officer got on the plane and said, 'They're not certain that they're going to issue you a visa to be able to stay here to give your speech tomorrow.'

"As it turned out," Graham chuckled, "they didn't attempt to enforce a visa requirement."

Graham was met at the airport by a Monroe County sheriff. "He indicated he had come in peace," Graham told the *Key West Citizen* that afternoon. "He told the Republican guard to hold their fire and he checked my passport and vaccination card. He was critical of the fact that I had no visa and then he issued me one and, in the event I was driving back, he gave me a border pass."

Following his meeting with the sheriff, Graham and his

entourage went to *La Lechónera* (now called *El Cacique*), one of Graham's favorite restaurants in Key West. "We spent the evening eating Cuban food, drinking beer, and adding to my speech the implications of the secession. One of the first things that came to mind was what a great foreign policy coup it was on behalf of the Reagan Administration. Without having fired a bullet or put any American at risk, we had been able to move the bearded dictator of Cuba an additional 40 miles further away from the United States.

"The secession happened to have occurred at the same time as the British-Argentine war over the Falkland Islands. So another thing we thought of that night was that it would be an appropriate first assignment for the foreign minister of the Conch Republic to go to London and Buenos Aires to try to become an intermediary in negotiating a settlement."

In a more serious vein the next day, following the commencement exercises, Graham said he felt the Border Patrol roadblock was "intolerable" and that the secession was a very "deft and appropriate" way of opposing it.

He added that the establishment of widely publicized checkpoints for drug smugglers and illegal aliens was indicative of "someone who had failed an IQ test."
Graham said he had not been told that the roadblock was going to be set up. The feds simply established it without so much as a "Hi there, guv, mind if we create a little

chaos in your state?"

"It was offensive to me and to the people in the Keys. And it wasn't a very effective tactic, if your goal was to cut off trafficking in illegal aliens and cocaine, because everybody knew where the station was. And unless you were the dumbest bunny in the Keys, you could figure out how to get around it."

When the roadblock was first brought to Graham's attention, ostensibly by Dennis Wardlow, he said he contacted the Justice Department in Washington and pressed for its removal, but got nowhere. At the time, he told the *Key West Citizen*: "The program is so obviously flawed that given a graceful way to retreat from the border station, the federal government will do so."

But two-and-a-half weeks later, the border station was still in business and being defended by Charles Rinkovech, coordinator of the vice-president's Task Force on Crime in Florida.

Speaking before a May 6 meeting of the Greater Key West Chamber of Commerce, Rinkovech said that 70 to 80 percent of the marijuana and cocaine that entered the United States came though south Florida. (He did not say that 150 pounds of marijuana were all the drugs that had been seized at the Florida City roadblock since its inception.) He added that the roadblock, which he called a "rational and legitimate law enforcement technique," was only part of a larger effort designed to curtail drugs, illegal aliens, and illegal machine guns, which he linked to violent crimes in Miami.

"There is a direct relationship between the import of drugs and violent crimes," he said. "There is a direct relationship between illegal aliens and violent crimes, and there is a direct relationship between illegal weapons and violent crime."

The task force came into the area, Rinkovech said, in response to an appeal from Miami Citizens Against Crime. He noted, however, that the federal government had limited authority and responsibility, and could not act on such crimes as murder, rape and robbery.

But, he said, by linking those crimes to drugs, aliens, and illegal weapons, the federal government could take action and have a "secondary effect" on violent crime.

He said the Border Patrol checkpoint was but part of an overall strategy to enforce the immigration laws of the U.S. "It was not designed to be an action by the Task Force to embarrass or inconvenience the Keys," he added. "The first day was a regrettable circumstance."

There had not been any more traffic back-ups since that first day, he said, and motorists were being delayed no more than five minutes at the most. He maintained, however, that the negative impact of violent crime in the area was having a far greater effect on tourism than the checkpoint in Florida City.

A thorough evaluation of the roadblock was going to

take place the following week, he added, but it was likely that it would continue on an "intermittent" basis.

Florida City: The Border Patrol and DEA agents staffing the roadblock were under siege.

"We were giving them a lot of hell," said Skeeter Dryer. "At that time, I was a re-enactor in the Confederate artillery. I had my own cannon here in the bar, a mountain howitzer, and we'd fire at them once in a while; just blow smoke at them. And we'd throw bricks of firecrackers under their trailer.

"The few people who went to the trouble to stop here were treated to the spirit of things, because we'd put up a black and white guardhouse out front. And we had guys marching back and forth with helmets on and old World War I rifles on their shoulders.

"Hell, we weren't doing any business, weren't making any money. We had to do something to keep from going crazy."

And the roadblock personnel eventually played along, Dryer added. "We had some laughs together. After they loosened up, they'd yell at me and threaten to arrest me for shooting my howitzer at them.

"My brother-in-law was here at the time, an Australian vacationing from Perth. We'd have to pass the checkpoint every evening to go home, and they'd always give him a rough time.

"I used to have an old dummy pirate that sat on a 100-

gallon fish tank in the bar. We'd put him in my convertible and the guys at the checkpoint would always demand to see his papers. We'd say, 'You're talking to a dummy, dummy!' and speed off.

"The Border Patrol and the others wouldn't come into my bar at first. But toward the end of the roadblock, some of the officers who had been imported from Texas started coming in. And when it was finally over, a lot of them stopped in and bought souvenir T-shirts, said good-bye, and apologized for all the trouble."

It ended this way:

The roadblock that had inconvenienced thousands of people, fostered a rebellion, attracted world-wide attention, embarrassed the federal government, and caused war to be declared on the United States was quietly dismantled late one night in June, a couple of months after it had been erected, and hauled away.

"It just disappeared," Dennis Wardlow said. "And that was the end of the whole big mess."

But it was only the beginning of the Conch Republic.

In the wake of the enormous amount of publicity generated by the secession came an avalanche of requests for Conch Republic souvenirs: flags, T-shirts, bumper stickers, currency, border passes, key chains, and passports, to name a few.

Also came hundreds of appeals for autographed photos of the leader of the world's newest nation, Prime Minister

Dennis Wardlow.

And letters and telegrams by the dozens poured into Key West's city hall, most shouting hurrah for the new Conch Republic.

One letter from an oral surgeon in Aurora, Illinois, offered his dental services to the military of the fledgling nation.

Two Colorado ladies wrote to say: "Have guns, will travel."

E.J. Karsh, a prisoner at the Big Pine Key Road Prison, volunteered without restriction his services, and the services of his fellow inmates, if Prime Minister Wardlow would merely commute their sentences.

A telegram from Virginia City, Nevada, said: "Due to the national emergency in Key West, the Comstock Air Force will back Mayor Dennis Wardlow with our full force and air power." It was signed Bruce Ladd, Colonel.

But to Wardlow the most important message came from Alice Wells, formerly a teacher at St. Joseph's Boys School in Key West. She praised him for putting on a good show and commended him for public service. Then she credited herself for the discipline she instilled in a seventh-grade student she had taught in the late '50s: a young man named Dennis Wardlow who would grow up to be the prime minister of an entire nation, albeit a very small one.

"I'm very proud of my role in the creation of the Conch Republic," Wardlow said in 1996. "And I'm pleased that so many people are still interested in it. I hope it's something that will live forever. I guess it represents my 15 minutes of fame."

As time passed, many of the accouterments of an authentic nation began to appear in the Conch Republic: Currency, stamps, a few anthems, a flag, official foods, flowers, and birds, even a national holiday.

The currency was worthless, souvenir coins that had been produced 10 years earlier, in 1972, for Key West's 150th anniversary. They were dug out of storage and circulated all over again for no reason anybody could come up with.

A commemorative stamp, also worthless, was designed by Postmaster Pasquale Goicoeches of Key Largo. "The turquoise- and flamingo-colored stamps will never carry your letter farther than your hand can reach without a 20-cent, U.S. stamp," he quipped to the *Keynoter* in 1982.

Disc jockeys in the Keys began to tout Stephen Sondheim's *Send in the Clowns* as the national anthem of the Conch Republic. This motivated musicians Brett Dolar and Jack Jones to compose and record a genuine anthem entitled the *Hymn of the Conch Republic*. But it didn't appeal to the eccentric disposition of Key Westers. It was too serious, too tame, too traditional and, therefore, got little air play in the "Land of the Loonies."

Many composers over the years set to music the events that led to Key West's secession, but none could please

Prime Minister Wardlow. In 1994, however, Wardlow finally received two tapes that surprised him, because he liked them both. He played the tapes for Key West's City Commissioners, who also liked them and declared them as official republic ballads. *The Conch Rebellion*, by Bobby Green, was named the republic's Battle Hymn and *The Conch Republic*, by MeriLynn and Joe Britz, was named the Official Song of the Conch Republic.

Be that as it may, in the hearts and minds of many people, including this Parrot Head, Key West *is Margaritaville*. Therefore, the national anthem of the Conch Republic, the unofficial national anthem, is Jimmy Buffett's Margaritaville—even though the song's lyrics have not a damned thing to do with anything pertaining to the Conch Republic and Buffett says *Margaritaville* may or may not be Key West.

Margaritaville is a "mythical island," Buffett writes in *Tales from Margaritaville* (Ballantine Books). "When you are there, you will know it."

The flag of the Conch Republic, a glorious thing to behold, was designed by a Conch and civil servant named Claude Valdez, also referred to by Prime Minister Wardlow as "the Betsy Ross of Key West." Valdez created the design in 1968 for a Chamber of Commerce-sponsored contest to choose a flag for Key West. The design won over 500 other entries and served as the official flag of the island city until the secession, when Valdez added

to it the words Conch Republic.

Now internationally famous, this proud symbol of Key West's fiercely independent nature consists of a blue banner with a flaming sun in its center. Above the sun are the words Conch Republic and centered within the sun is a pink and white conch shell. Stars representing the northern and southern constellations are located in the banner's lower left and upper right corners, along with the words Key West and the year in which the city was incorporated, 1828.

Conch chowder, conch fritters, and Key Lime pie became the official foods of the new nation. Hibiscus was proclaimed the national flower. And residents split into two warring camps over which should be the national bird—the pelican or the frigate bird. This momentous controversy has never been settled.

The national holiday of the Conch Republic is, of course, its Independence Day, which now occurs in the midst of a wild, uproarious, 10-day celebration called Conch Republic Days.

"It's a party I throw for 20,000 people every year," said Peter Anderson, the Secretary-General of the Conch Republic and organizer of the annual blowout since 1990, when it almost succumbed to indifference. But more about that later.

The early celebrations of Key West's independence were attended primarily by a few hundred locals and consisted of immature versions of some of today's events.

The second anniversary of the Conch Republic, for example, began with a five-block-long parade along Duval Street. Today, that event is billed as the "World's Longest Parade," because it starts on the Atlantic Ocean-end of Duval and finishes at the opposite end of the mile-long street, at the Gulf of Mexico.

The parade was followed by a bed race. Each of three elaborately decorated beds on wheels was pushed by four runners down Duval Street in pursuit of cash and prizes. These days, as many as 48 runners with a dozen beds might compete in the dopey derby.

On a flatbed trailer in front of the Chamber of Commerce, where the secession took place in 1982, ministers of the Republic's current government reaffirmed its sovereignty with a flag-raising ceremony. Then a monu-

The site of the seccession is now marked
by a monument.

ment was dedicated to the founding fathers and heroes of
the Conch Republic.

A bronze plaque on the coral limestone monument
reads as follows:

*On April 18, 1982, at the head of the highway out of the
Florida Keys, the United States Border Patrol established a
roadblock. For the first time in the United States' history, an
entire section of the country was officially treated as a foreign
land. Returning travelers were required to prove United States
citizenship and subjected to forced searches.*

*At noon on April 23, 1982, the Island of Key West, in a
mock ceremony, declared its independence from the United
States by naming ministers of the new nation which it called*

'The Conch Republic' and by hoisting its own flag.

Founding Fathers: Dennis Wardlow, Dennis Bitner, William E. Smith, Edwin O. Swift III, Townsend Kieffer, John Magliola.

Dedicated April 25, 1986, by Prime Minister and Mayor Tom Sawyer.

Later that afternoon there was a conch fritter-tossing contest for children. And the second annual celebration of Key West's independence came to an end with a ball at a waterfront cafe.

The popularity of Conch Republic Days neither increased nor decreased much over the next few years. It was an event for locals and they liked it that way, because they had to work for and put up with tourist revelers all the rest of the time.

But the work of nurturing the fledgling nation continued. During the Conch Republic's 1987 celebration of its symbolic secession, Tom Sawyer, who was then prime minister, made a weighty announcement, according to a UPI report. Seeking an international forum for his tiny "country's" eccentric voice, he had applied for membership in the United Nations.

In a letter to U.N. Secretary-General Javier Perez de Cuellar, Sawyer, who also served as Key West's mayor, said the Conch Republic would "add to the General Assembly's deliberations a voice of goodwill and good humor, which has not been overly prevalent among members in some years."

In keeping with his country's offbeat humor, Sawyer reminded Perez de Cuellar that "foremost among individual freedoms recognized in the Conch Republic is the freedom to enjoy life to its utmost.

"It is indeed unfortunate," Sawyer wrote, "that some U.N. members seem to have disregarded this freedom in their national priorities, but we believe it is well worth representing as a global goal for people everywhere."

And what was Perez de Cuellar's response to Sawyer's petition? Nada. There wasn't any. The secretary-general rudely ignored him.

But the slap that *really* hurt came three years later, in 1990, from so-called friendly hands. Organizers from Key West's Association for Tourist Development, the group that had been producing Conch Republic Days, decided to drop the celebration like a hot conch fritter.

"They decided that it didn't put enough heads on beds (bring in enough tourists) and, therefore, wasn't worth celebrating anymore," said Peter Anderson, who had moved to Key West from New York 1985. "But Rear Admiral Finbar (Captain Finbar Gittelman, Rear Admiral and Commander of the Conch Republic fleet, which consisted entirely of the 74-foot schooner *Wolf*) and several others, to whom the Conch Republic was nearer and dearer than they imagined, decided that we could not let our nation's eighth anniversary go uncelebrated. We could not stand by and let a tradition of celebrating our sovereignty in a public and notorious manner be broken. So we started a new Conch Republic independence celebration, made a new statement of our individuality, our uniqueness, our independent spirit. And for my efforts I was appointed (by then-mayor Captain Tony Tarracino) as Secretary-General of the Conch Republic and have been carrying on in that capacity ever since with some vigor."

Indeed he has. Shortly after becoming the Conch Republic's Secretary-General and "chief bureaucrat," Anderson fired off a letter to his counterpart at the U.N. "I'm writing to ascertain the proper procedures for admission of our tiny island nation into the community of nations," he wrote. "Due to the increasingly enlightened situation worldwide, we feel it is time to take our rightful place amongst the nations of the world."

Noting the feisty island's "don't tread on me" attitude at the time of secession, Anderson said the Conch Republic would offer a "different viewpoint" to the United Nations.

And Perez de Cuellar's response? The same one he gave Sawyer—ill-mannered silence.

Anderson sent Perez de Cuellar yet another request for membership guidelines in 1991, and made the same request of the secretary-general's successor, Boutros-Boutros Ghali, in 1994. Both were ignored.

"We're being stonewalled," Anderson said in 1996. "We have been writing letters to them since 1990, requesting only that they forward to us the guidelines for applying for membership in the United Nations, but so far we've been resoundingly ignored."

And whatever became of Prime Minister Wardlow's 1982 request for $1 billion in foreign aid?

"We're still waiting for it," Anderson replied. "In fact, during the recent shutdown of the government, I faxed out to the world press that we expected our foreign aid would be further delayed, but since we've been waiting 14 years, a few more weeks won't matter."

Does being ignored by the U.N. and United States government make Anderson angry? Not according Key West writer John Guerra. In *Florida Keys Magazine* (April 1994), Guerra said, "This is what he likes to do. It is in the spirit of the Conch Republic's motto: 'Our glorious mission is the mitigation of world tension through the exercise of humor.'"

(That's Motto Number Two, actually. Motto Number One, Anderson said, is "We seceded where others failed." He coined them both, he added proudly.)

But we're getting ahead of ourselves. More of Anderson's political high jinks in a moment. First, let's back up briefly to 1990 when the self-described "corporate animal, builder, carpenter, plumber, electrician, cabinet maker, furniture maker, boat designer, boat builder, general

The Schooner Wharf Bar, headquarters of the Conch Republic
Independence Day celebration

contractor, writer, and loose cannon" took over the production of Conch Republic Days from the faithless
Association for Tourist Development. He and his loyalist
investors lost $6,000 on the festival, mostly on two expen-
sive and poorly attended events, the Ambassador's Ball and
the Last Tango on Tank Island Beach Party.

"They were logistical nightmares," Anderson told *The
Miami Herald*. "Great parties, though." Which in the final
analysis is all that really matters in Key West.

Things are quite different today, however. Because of
Anderson's inexhaustible and facile promotion of the
Conch Republic and its annual independence celebration,
it is attended by over 20,000 "heads on beds" who spend

money with Key West abandon. They also flock to such loopy events as "The World's Longest Parade," "The World's Longest Party," "The Conch Republic Horn Blowing Contest," "The Conch Republic Naval Parade & The Great Battle for the Conch Republic," "The Victory Party and Official Surrender Ceremony at the Schooner Wharf Bar," "The Island 107 Conch Republic Bed Race," the "Tales of the Old Conch Republic Poetry Slam," and "The Grand Ambassador's Costume Ball"—which now is a money-maker.

Still, Anderson is not an island hero. He has a number of detractors who condemn him for going too far in commercializing the Conch Republic and for taking his "imaginary post" as Secretary-General too seriously.

Now, I ask you, do these sound like the words of a man who takes his job too seriously?

"By virtue of adverse possession statutes under international law, and because we have celebrated our independence in a public and notorious manner for more than seven years, unchallenged by the United States, we are, in fact, a sovereign nation. We have our own passports and diplomats who have been welcomed all over the world. Accepting a foreign diplomat into your country is a formal recognition of the diplomat's country under international law. By that standard, we've been recognized by Sweden, Russia, France, Monaco, Ireland, Spain, Mexico, Ecuador, 13 Caribbean countries, and the United States of

America. And we now have Conch-sulates in Switzerland, New Orleans, Maine, and Havana."

Further evidence of the seriousness with which Anderson takes his job is revealed in an undated press release from his "official office."

"As the world's first, 'fifth-world' country," says the release, "we exist as a 'state of mind' and aspire only to bring more warmth, humor, and respect to a planet we find in sore need of all three."

When the serious-minded Anderson found out about President Bill Clinton's announcement of the Summit of the Americas, which was going to be held in Miami in December of 1994, he decided the event would benefit from some of the Conch Republic's unique political philosophy. But Alexander Almasov of the U.S. State Department didn't agree. He said the Conch Republic was not a country and, therefore, was not invited to attend the summit.

Nevertheless, Anderson and the rest of the grimly determined delegation from the Conch Republic—which included gazillionaire Mel Fisher, who had found the fabulous treasure of the 16th century Spanish galleon *Nuestra Senora de Atocha* in 1985—succeeded not only in attending the summit, but in making their august presence felt by hosting a number of political bigwigs in the Hotel Inter-Continental's $2,600-a-night Royal Suite. It was one of only two suites—the other was the $3,000-a-night

Presidential Suite—that had not been booked for dele-
gates by the State Department . "They were unequal
accommodations, which made them diplomatically incor-
rect," Anderson explained.

The plucky Conch Republicans also succeeded in over-
coming the media ban that the State Department had
imposed on them and were interviewed by Reuters, The
Associated Press, CNN, and the stuffy *London Financial
Times*, among other international news media.

"The Conch Republic's message of humor, warmth, and
respect could not be suppressed," Anderson said.

The Secretary-General next took his job too seriously a
year later, in December of 1995. That was when the U.S.
Government again infuriated Key Westers by closing Fort
Jefferson National Park in the wake of a federal shutdown.

"It was causing our tour operators to lose $30,000 a
day," Anderson said, "so the Conch Republic immediately went to work to reopen the park with Conch
Republic money."

To accomplish this munificent goal, Anderson and others planned to "invade" the park, which is located in the
isolated Dry Tortugas, 70 miles southwest of Key West.
First, three antique biplanes were going to bomb the fort
with the Conch Republic's customary weapon, stale Cuban
bread. Then troops from the Key West Seaplane and the
Yankee Freedom/Tortugas Ferry were going to go ashore,
give the park's manager a check for $1,600 (the cost of

operating the park for a day), and declare the park to be open. But the invasion plan collapsed when ill-humored park officials decided to play hardball.

The seaplane and ferry, which regularly brought tourists to the fort, were threatened with the loss of their commercial operating permits if they entered park waters, Anderson explained. Also, he said there was some concern expressed about the effect of stale Cuban bread on the fort's serious rat problem. "They didn't want them to grow any fatter."

A privately-owned and -operated seaplane, which had no commercial license to lose, was then commandeered by the Conch Republic forces. Anderson, a couple of other dignitaries, and some reporters were flown to Fort Jefferson, and Anderson tried to give Park Manager Wayne Landrum the $1,600 check.

Landrum said he could not accept the money and urged Anderson to offer it to the park department through proper channels. Anderson agreed to do so, then asked to be issued a citation for entering an area that had been closed by a federal shutdown. And Landrum reluctantly complied.

The citation was needed, Anderson explained, as evidence in a legal action by the Conch Republic to require the federal government, in the event of future shutdowns, to accept foreign aid from the Republic for the operation of Fort Jefferson.

Representing the Conch Republic in this action was, of

course, David Paul Horan, who was also Secretary of the Conch Republic Air Forces, which then consisted of only one aircraft, his own.

One last, comically sensational tale about how seriously Anderson and many other Conch Republic ministers have taken their "imaginary" posts:

September 1996: Secretary-General Anderson received warning that the Conch Republic was about to be invaded by the 478th Civil Affairs Battalion of the United States Army Reserve.

"I immediately called the Prime Minister (Wardlow) and said, 'Mr. Prime Minister, the U.S. Army is invading the Conch Republic in a training exercise to simulate a geographically isolated foreign nation,'" Anderson said. "'And this is being done without any prior consultation with our government. How do you want to handle this?' And he said, 'Well, Mr. Secretary, I'm leaving on four days of much-needed R & R (rest and recreation) ... So, I'm placing the country in your hands with full faith and confidence in your ability to defend the Republic.'"

The empowered Anderson abruptly called WOZN, "the official radio station of the Conch Republic," and asked its on-air personnel to alert the citizenry of the "grave situation" it was facing.

He then wrote a letter objecting to the impending "incursion" as an affront to the sovereignty of the Conch Republic and to its hospitality, and air-mailed it to

President Clinton, with copies to the Joint Chiefs of Staff and Secretary of State Warren Christopher.

"We assured the president that, while we found this incursion lacking in humor and respect, we would find appropriately funny ways to repel it," Anderson wrote in "The Battle for the Conch Republic," an article for the *Key West Citizen*.

That evening, Anderson convened a meeting of the "war cabinet" at the Schooner Wharf Bar. It was presided over by a cherished legend in Key West, the Supreme Commander of the Armed Forces, Admiral Wilhelmina (Willi) Harvey. Born in 1912, Mrs. Harvey is a fourth-generation conch and an unbeatable politician. She had served as the first female mayor of Monroe County and served "I forget how many terms," she said, as a Monroe County Commissioner. So popular a candidate is she that, when she ran for re-election in 1996, nobody ran against her.

Also in attendance at the meeting were Rear Admiral Finbar, Conch Republic Air Force General Freddy Cabanas, and Rob and Roxanne Kunkel, the founding members of InterConch, a "top-secret, intelligence-gathering organization."

"We hatched a battle plan to deal with the unauthorized incursion of the 478th," Anderson said.

The plan called first for General Cabanas to "soften up" the Army convoy as it crossed the Boca Chica Bridge by bombing it with the usual stale Cuban bread. Then the plan called for Admiral Harvey, Rear Admiral Finbar, and the militia to meet the "invaders" at the Stock Island Bridge and prevent them from entering the capital city of Key West.

To prepare for its defense, the Conch Republic's munitions factory, La Dichosa Bakery, began working overtime to produce that most terrifying of weapons, stale Cuban Bread.

("Though deadly, stale Cuban bread is not covered by the Geneva Protocols of 1925, nor the Hague Conventions of 1899."—Susana Bellido, *The Miami Herald*.)

"Their commendable performance in the face of the threat to our sovereignty will never be forgotten," Anderson said of La Dichosa's employees. "Baking far into the night and the wee hours of the morning, they produced a formidable quantity of ammunition."

More about this historic event from Anderson's "Battle for the Conch Republic":

"Meanwhile, the 478th was starting to wonder what they had gotten themselves into. At 9:45 p.m. a Major Muller was on the phone trying to talk his way out of a full-scale war. He explained that they were the 'good guys,' were not here to harm us, and hoped confrontation could be avoided. It was explained to him that our plans were ... immutable, and that they would be repelled if they refused to meet our demands at the border of the capital. The Major requested a copy of our demands, which were faxed to him as we talked. Upon review, the Major felt that our demands were acceptable. At 10:50 p.m. we received a fax from the 478th stating that they 'had in no way meant to challenge or impugn the sovereignty of the Conch Republic.'

"The United States Army had acknowledged the sovereignty of the Conch Republic!

"Even though the battle was now to be ceremonial, by Friday morning all was in readiness. WOZN had been on full emergency broadcast and the citizenry was alerted and enthusiastic. InterConch was in position. The Air Force was ready. Admiral Harvey was in uniform and in command. Key West Lager had agreed to provide the beer. The Key West Police Department and the Sheriff's Department had been alerted to expect an incident, and the 478th was rolling.

"Over 200 citizens and members of the Navy, Air Force, and militia were crowded at the foot of the bridge. InterConch kept Command and Control constantly advised of the whereabouts of the lead elements of the 478th, in spite of the fact that they were taking fire from the Conch Republic Air Force as they crossed the Boca Chica Bridge.

"As the 478th rolled onto the Stock Island Bridge, the Armed Forces of the Conch Republic sallied forth, led by

Admiral Harvey and Rear Admiral Finbar, and stopped the lead vehicle of the 478th dead in its tracks. Major Kim Hooper dismounted and approached the Admiral. They were introduced. Admiral Harvey read him our list of demands, including her request for him to ask permission to enter our country. He accepted all our demands with a very polite, 'Yes, Ma'am.'

"At that point, a mighty blast of the Queen Conch shell and a ceremonial blast of the *Wolf's* cannon welcomed the gentlemen and ladies of the 478th onto our island.

"We had won!"

Laughter!

Cheers!

Applause!

Almost everybody in Key West enjoyed that daring exploit of the Conch Republic's troops all the way down to their flip-flops, as did the news media *and* the members of the Army's 478th Civil Affairs Battalion. Secretary-General Peter Anderson, Admiral Wilhelmina Harvey, Rear Admiral Finbar Gittelman, Air Force Secretary David Paul Horan, General Freddy Cabanas, InterConch operatives Rob and Roxanne Kunkel, and all the rest of the Republic's "imaginary" ministers and militia had once again taken their jobs too seriously and made us chuckle. They were heroes and heroines for a day. Well, for 15 minutes anyway. And had there been a popularity poll,

Anderson would have probably rated right up there with the Macarena, the dance craze *du jour*.

But then, five months later, Anderson's popularity was in the toilet. He was being damned by a horde of rabid Key Westers, skewered by the media, and the city commissioners were disavowing association with his corporation, The Conch Republic Inc., which organizes the annual independence celebration, sells passports to the fanciful island nation for $23.95, and confers ambassadorships and other republic titles.

Here's why:

Anderson finally took his job too seriously—*for real*, according to a number of accounts. Cloaked in the flag of the Conch Republic, he went to Tallahassee and stood before Governor Lawton Chiles and his cabinet, who were considering the approval of the Florida Keys National Marine Sanctuary—a super-hot and divisive issue in the Keys. Anderson then charged that the Sanctuary was nothing but camouflage for a conspiracy on the part of The Nature Conservancy and certain federal and state agencies to force Keys residents to sell their land to the Conservancy at below-market prices. And then, in the name of the Conch Republic, he declared war on the Conservancy and Marine Sanctuary. The Conservancy later denied the accusation, labeling it a "complete and total lie"

In more general and emotional terms, Anderson misappropriated the name, flag, and spirit of the Conch Republic for truly serious political purposes. And in doing so he upset the delicate balance between seriousness and silliness that Key Westers feel *must* be maintained in all Conch Republic endeavors.

City Commissioner Henry Bethel said Anderson's declaration of war was part of a money-making scheme that reflected poorly on Key West and its citizens. "I've gotten nothing but bad calls over this," he told the *Key West Citizen* (January 31). "And every citizen I've talked to says the Conch Republic belongs to all of us, not just Peter Anderson, who's trying to make a buck."

Anderson claimed he represented the 54.5 percent of Keys voters who opposed the Sanctuary in a non-binding referendum on November. 5. "As Secretary-General of the Conch Republic, I am bound by duty to side with the voice of the Keys and fight the abuses of regulatory and legal actions perpetrated by our government in collusion with The Nature Conservancy.

"The Conch Republic is always going to celebrate its fun and frivolity. But when its people are threatened and government does nothing, it will respond."

A broadside on January 23 from David Ethridge, editor of the weekly *Solares Hill*: "Dear Peter: Stick with your tried and true Conch Republic schtick. Forget the politics. The act isn't flying, no one's laughing, it's an embarrassment."

Former Key West mayor Captain Tony Tarracino rose to Anderson's defense on January 31. "He saved the Conch Republic from extinction," he told the *Miami Herald*. "People like Peter are needed in Key West. If he's making money, he's like anyone else. He's trying to survive."

The debate reached a head on February 4, when the City Commission voted unanimously on a resolution to disavow association between the political positions of the Conch Republic Inc. and those of the city. Commissioners said they were embarrassed by Anderson's recent activities and angry that he had incorporated Conch Republic, with himself as president and CEO.

"This was a fun thing that accomplished a mission," Mayor Dennis Wardlow told the *Miami Herald* (February 6). "I don't want to see it become a private industry."

Some commissioners suggested that the city should seize control of the republic and make the secretary-general's post a rotating, two-year appointment, or a fund-raising honor.

Anderson did not attend the meeting, but faxed a letter urging the commissioners to pass the resolution. He said it would be better if the relationship between the city and the republic were clearly defined.

But the fleet commander of the Conch Republic Navy asked the city not to renounce the republic.

"I realize that the city government and the Conch Republic are not the same thing. But you are the leaders of our community, which is the Conch Republic," said Rear Admiral Finbar Gittelman, captain of the republic's flagship, the schooner *Wolf*. "I don't want it in business or in politics, either. That's not what it's for. I just don't want to see it go away."

And it never will, faithful readers. The Conch Republic can't go away because it now lives by faith and, therefore, its spirit will continue to survive unchanged through times of abuse and diminishment and neglect. Despite faultfinders, opportunists, and demagogues, it will remain what its founding fathers intended it to be: a wonderfully bizarre place in our hearts and minds where we can go when we're sore in need of one of the most uplifting things that life has to offer—a good laugh.

Long live the Conch Republic!

©Wright Langley

Admiral Wilhelmina Harvey, Supreme Commander of the Armed Forces of the Conch Republic, and Art Mosley, a former city planner, embody the spirit of the Conch Republic.

ADDENDUM: 1998

"Nothing's over 'til the
fat lady sings."

—Groucho Marx

In the Marx Brothers' 1935, MGM film "A Night at the Opera," Chico Marx, forced to watch a performance of *Il Trovatore*, prematurely expresses relief that the ordeal is finally over. His brother Groucho turns to him, points with his cigar to the hefty contralto played by Margaret Dumont and says, "Nothing's over 'til the fat lady sings."

Well, patient reader, the same holds true for this eccentric chronicle. The fat lady hasn't sung, so it isn't over yet, regardless of how badly you may want it to be. There are still—a year after the first printing of this book—a few things you need to know, some of which pertain to your palate. So pay close attention for just a few more paragraphs.

First, the fate of Peter Anderson, the erratic Secretary-General of the Conch Republic:

When last we saw Anderson, in February 1997, he and his business, Conch Republic Inc., were being threatened with disenfranchisement by certain of Key West's city commissioners; this because of political behavior they deemed to be inappropriate and embarrassing, and because they felt Anderson was claiming rights of ownership to the name of the fanciful Conch Republic to protect his business of selling passports and organizing the annual Conch Republic Independence Celebration.

Didn't happen.

At one of the most absurd meetings in the history of the city commission, on March 18, 1997, Anderson butted heads with Commissioner Henry Bethel, champion of a resolution to restrict the term of the fictional title and office of Secretary-General of the Conch Republic to one year. Anderson said his appointment as Secretary-General, made by former Key West mayor Capt. Tony Tarracino, was for life, then claimed that the resolution would encourage the city to expropriate the Conch Republic Independence Celebration.

"What this is about is that they're trying to steal what is mine!" Anderson shouted. "They're trying to deprive me of my living! I put many years of hard work into this Conch Republic. If I did something you thought embarrassed you, that's my right.!"

Anderson then said he was "going to go about my business anyway." And then he declared his candidacy for mayor, vowing to fight "citywide corruption."

"This whole thing is pretty silly," City Commissioner Sally Lewis said later. "This is not a real world we're talking about. These are not real jobs. If Peter wants to call himself God, he can call himself whatever he wants. I don't care."

"This is ridiculous," echoed Mayor Wardlow, who, with Lewis, wound up opposing the resolution. Nevertheless,

Commissioner Bethel and commissioners Carmen Turner, Percy Curry, and Merili McCoy made sure the measure was approved.

But then, in a jarring and bizarre turn-around, the commissioners unanimously supported a resolution to participate in the Conch Republic Independence Celebration.

"Then let's get on with the party and the fun," Anderson responded. "Thank you very much."

As for Anderson's contention in the race to become Mayor of Key West and Prime Minister of the Conch Republic, all at the same time:

Didn't win.

Didn't even make the run-offs.

But the agony of defeat was soothed by a major victory in another arena. The Conch Republic Independence Celebration of 1997 was a rip-snorting success. "The marketplace and the citizenry spoke most eloquently during the celebration," Anderson crowed. "More events than ever, more sponsorships than ever, more community participation than ever, fuller hotels and airplanes than ever, bigger, better, busier, funner, funnier. Oh, yes, the marketplace spoke loudly and clearly. 'We love Anderson!'"

Although not as much, perhaps, as Anderson seems to love himself.

Now, the fate of Dennis Wardlow, a founding father of the Conch Republic and four-term mayor of Key West:

His Honor wielded the gavel of authority for the last

time at a city commission meeting on October 21, 1997. Then he walked out of the old City Hall on Greene St. and into his future as the owner-operator of Isle of Dreams Inc., a houseboat rental company. And he didn't look back. After 25 years of service, many of which were tumultuous and painful, Wardlow said he was damned glad to go.

Enough of politics—"A dog's life without dog's decencies," Kipling called them—and on to better things for the soul!

Throughout these pages you have encountered comestibles which may be foreign to you. Two of them, Key Lime pie and conch fritters, are official foods of the Conch Republic. Cuban bread, *stale* Cuban bread, is, of course, the republic's weapon of choice. And the *Cuba Libre*, the drink of liberty, is the favorite lubricant of many of the Conch Republic's loyal subjects. All are extraordinarily pleasing to the palate and to the soul, and you must experience each of them if you really want to know Key West.

So, bring out your pots and pans and cheapest glassware. Put on your oldest T-shirt, your cut-offs, Ray-Bans, flip-flops, and your favorite Jimmy Buffett album, and follow these recipes to the letter:

KEY LIME PIE

This is a sacred delicacy in Key West—sacred!—and it must be made with Key Limes, or it's not Key Lime pie.

Key Limes, unlike the green, thick-skinned, lemon-shaped "limes" that are sold in supermarkets everywhere, are small, yellow, thin-skinned, and almost perfectly round. They are much more sour than their larger green cousins and, unfortunately, difficult to come by. There were groves of them throughout the keys during the 1920s, but they were wiped out by a hurricane in 1926 and never replanted. Now, the only remaining grove of Key Limes is on Matecumbe Key.

Legend has it that Key Lime pie was first concocted at the Tradewinds Boarding House in the early 1940s for a frequent visitor named Tennessee Williams, who purchased a home in Key West in 1949.

INGREDIENTS

1   9-inch, graham cracker pie crust (or make one from scratch, if you're a purist)

1   14-ounce can of sweetened, condensed milk

3   egg yolks

1/2   cup of fresh Key Lime juice (or use Nellie & Joe's Famous Key West Lime Juice from concentrate, which is available in gourmet shops, or from Nellie and Joe's, P.O. Box 2368, Key West, FL 33045)

1/2   teaspoon of grated Key Lime peel (optional)

2   cups of whipped cream

HOW TO

Combine condensed milk, egg yolks, lime juice, and lime peel. Blend until smooth. Pour filling into pie crust and bake at 350 degrees for 10 minutes. Allow to stand for 10 minutes, then refrigerate. Just before serving, top with whipped cream and garnish with very thin slices of Key Lime.

Taste and know Paradise.

CONCH FRITTERS

Some people say conch fritters were invented in the Bahamas in the 1700s. Others swear they were invented in Key West 100 years later. But almost everyone agrees that conch fritters are marvelous things to nibble and, when stale, make excellent missiles, although not nearly the missiles that stale Cuban bread makes, as you already know.

There are two ways to make conch fritters—the wrong way and the right way. The wrong way is to whip up a batch of corn bread batter, mix in some conch and a few other traditional ingredients, roll the batter into golf-ball-sized balls and fry it. This results not in conch fritters, but in lowly hush puppies merely disguised as conch fritters; heavy, grainy little grease sponges that feel like they swell up in your stomach and take forever to finally dissolve and pass into oblivion.

The exalted conch fritter, on the other hand, is a light, piquant, slightly chewy, and easily digested morsel about

the size and shape of a teaspoon. Following is a thorough-
ly non-traditional but deliciously effective way of making
the little goodies. And if you deviate in any way from this
recipe, you will fail miserably in capturing the essence of
the conch fritter as Neptune and Betty Crocker intended
it to be.

INGREDIENTS

1/2 pound of minced conch, which is usually available
only at specialty seafood stores. If you've ever seen a
conch, however, you may wish to substitute an
equal amount of clams, which are not nearly so fright-
ful-looking and actually taste better than conch.
But don't tell anybody you've made this substitution,
because then you'll have to admit that you've made
clam fritters, which may result in ridicule.

1   medium onion
1   small green pepper
2   tablespoons of crushed red pepper
1/2 tablespoon of salt
1/4 teaspoon of thyme
1   clove of garlic
2   tablespoons of Tabasco sauce if you're a wuss,
     more if you're a real woman or man
2   cups of Betty Crocker's Bisquick, but deny that
     you've used it
1   egg   *Continued...*

1/4   cup of milk, added a teaspoon at a time
3   Key Limes, or some Key Lime juice
      Peanut oil

HOW TO

Combine in a food processor the conch (or clams), onion, green pepper, red pepper, salt, thyme, garlic, and Tabasco sauce, and hit the Mince button for a few seconds. Then add the egg and hit the button again.

Now, put the Bisquick into a large bowl and dig out a little hollow in the middle of it, so it looks like a mini-volcano. OK? Now, pour all the stuff listed above into the hollow and stir, adding small amounts of milk as necessary to create a mixture that's about the consistency of very thick pancake batter.

Heat the peanut oil (preferably in a deep-fryer, but a skillet will do) on medium-high until it reaches a temperature of about 350 degrees. Don't test the oil by sticking your finger into it. Test it by dropping a small amount of the batter into it. If the batter floats and puffs up, the oil is hot enough to do the job.

Now, start dropping half-teaspoons of the batter into the hot oil. When they're puffy and golden brown, remove them with a slotted spoon and drain on paper towels, or old money, whichever is handiest. Serve with Key Lime slices, cocktail sauce, and honey mustard to six people you really like and want to please.

CUBAN BREAD

Sorry, but you're not going to get the recipe for Cuban Bread (*Pan Cubano*). The reason is, it's too complicated to make. It requires too much work and too much skill. And I know you well enough by now to know that you're not up to it.

However, you do need to know these distinguishing characteristics of Cuban bread:

- It's usually lighter and crispier than French bread, because it's made with water, instead of milk, and with "active" or "fast-rising" yeast, instead of— what?—"inactive, slow-rising" yeast?
- It's tastier than French bread, because bay leaves are imbedded in its top before baking.
- Most Cuban bakeries prepare it in awesome loaves that are at least three feet long.
- And when it becomes stale, which doesn't take long, it acquires the texture and heft of balsa wood.

If you want to partake of this delectable creation, go to Key West, if you're not already there, and then go to 1206 White Street. That's address of La Dichosa Bakery, which is also the munitions factory of the Conch Republic.

CUBA LIBRE

The name means Free Cuba! And the drink was formulated in 1898 at the Floridita, a popular bar and restaurant in Havana which became Ernest Hemingway's favorite haunt in the mid-1940s. The drink's formulator was not a Cuban, but Thomas Minnewit, an American reporter for William Randolph Hearst's *New York Journal*. He was in Cuba, covering the Spanish-American War, and had brought with him one of the drink's key ingredients—Coca-Cola.

HOW TO

Put the juice of half a Key Lime (or common green lime, if you really must) into a cheap glass, along with a sliver of the lime's peel. You'll want to use a cheap glass so you can down the drink, shout "Free Cuba!" then shatter glass on the floor, as was the custom of the habitués of the Floridita in 1898. Add two ounces of dark rum, preferably Cuban rum (which presently is illegal), some ice cubes, then fill the remainder of the glass with Coke. The result is a libation that will free you from all your earthly inhibitions and make you a legend in your own mind.

OK, that's it. No more recipes, no more off-the-wall personalities, no more political absurdities, nada.

Your time is appreciated. We hope you feel that it has been well spent and that, sooner or later, you'll spend even more of it—physically or spiritually—in the Conch Republic.

And, now, please welcome the fat lady, who will sing about "wastin' away again in Margaritaville."

Gregory King is a journalist, screenwriter, and partner in the Lexington, Kentucky-based marketing firm of Calvert & King. However, he can often be found wastin' away at the Schooner Wharf Bar in the Conch Republic. His E-mail address is gwking@lex.infi.net.